Marvel

Bibbidi–bobbidi–boo,
this book belongs to you.

Marvel

For information regarding permission, write to:
Disney Licensed Publishing, 114 Fifth Avenue, New York, New York 10011.

978-0-545-08626-4   0-545-08626-4
Printed in the U.S.A.   First printing, May 2008

SCHOLASTIC INC.
New York   Toronto   London   Auckland   Sydney
Mexico City   New Delhi   Hong Kong   Buenos Aires

inderella couldn't be happier. Her dreams had finally come true. With the help of her fairy godmother and her special mice friends, Cinderella had made it to the ball where she had met the Prince. It was love at first sight! The couple soon married, and Cinderella became a princess.

Cinderella went to live in the palace, leaving behind her wicked stepmother and two cruel stepsisters, Anastasia and Drizella. All three of them had treated Cinderella like a servant. Now the sisters were angry and jealous of Cinderella because they had to do their own chores.

Secretly, Anastasia yearned for a happy ending of her own.

One day, she spotted Cinderella and the Prince walking towards the woods. Anastasia followed them to a clearing where Cinderella's friends had planned a surprise anniversary party. Anastasia hid behind a tree and watched.

With a swish of her wand, the Fairy
Godmother said, "Bibbidi-bobbidi-boo!" Instantly,
the clothes Cinderella and the Prince were
wearing transformed into the ball costumes they
had worn the night they had fallen in love.

Anastasia gasped. "So that's how Cinderella
did it—*magic*!"

As the mice and the Fairy Godmother
serenaded the beautiful couple, the Prince lovingly
took Cinderella in his arms. The couple danced in
the moonlight.

The Fairy Godmother was having so much fun
that she threw her arms up in excitement, sending
her wand flying through the air. The wand landed
right in front of Anastasia!

"Perfect!" cried Anastasia. She snatched the wand and ran.

Anastasia hurried home to her mother and sister. Just then the Fairy Godmother appeared.

"Child, put that down," the Fairy Godmother scolded Anastasia. "In the wrong hands that wand could be extremely dangerous."

Anastasia refused. She turned the Fairy Godmother into a stone garden gnome!

The wicked Stepmother's eyes grew wide when she saw the power of the wand. "Do you realize what this means, girls? It means power, riches . . . *revenge*," she said.

Then the Stepmother pointed the wand towards the sky. "Reverse the moon and sun. Turn back tide and time. Unravel Cinderella's happily ever after to the moment my troubles began!"

Suddenly time turned back to the exact moment that the Grand Duke arrived at the manor with a single glass slipper. The lucky girl whose foot fit the slipper would marry the Prince.

Just before Anastasia tried on the glass slipper, her mother used the magic wand to stretch the shoe to fit on her daughter's big foot.

The Grand Duke was stunned. "It fits?"

"It fits!" cried Anastasia.

"I hereby declare that we have found the Prince's bride-to-be," announced the Duke. "We must return to the palace at once."

Just then Cinderella appeared at the top of the stairs, holding the matching glass slipper. "No! It can't be," she said, looking very upset.

The Stepmother confronted Cinderella. "Whatever you think happened last night was a dream," the wicked woman said icily. Then she took Cinderella's glass slipper and dropped it over the staircase, shattering the shoe.

Cinderella's mice friends, Jaq and Gus, did
their best to cheer her up. If only Cinderella could
see the Prince again, everything would be set
right. The three friends hurried to the palace.

Getting into the palace wouldn't be easy, however. Cinderella pretended to be a servant delivering a wheel of cheese to the King. Gus and Jaq hid in her pocket.

Once inside, the friends split up and went to look for the Prince.

The mice found the Prince first. But they were too late. They watched as Cinderella's Stepmother used the magic wand to cast a spell on the Prince.

Suddenly the Prince thought Anastasia was his true love. The Prince asked Anastasia to marry him.

"We have to find Cinderelly!" Jaq exclaimed to Gus.

Cinderella found the Prince a little while later. Sadly, he didn't remember her at all. He spoke only of Anastasia. He planned to marry her that very night.

Cinderella was devastated. She didn't know what to do.

Luckily, the mice knew the truth. Once they found Cinderella, they explained what they had seen.

Stunned, Cinderella uttered, "She made him forget who I am." More determined than ever, Cinderella declared, "Boys, we have to get that wand!"

Meanwhile, the King took Anastasia aside. He handed her a small box with a simple seashell inside.

"This shell was the Queen's most treasured possession," the King explained. "The day we met, you see, we reached for it at the same moment. When our hands touched, that's when I knew I had found true love."

"You knew that just by touching her hand?" asked Anastasia.

"There's no more powerful force in the world than true love," the King told her.

Back inside the palace, Cinderella watched her stepmother and stepsisters through a keyhole as the Stepmother locked the wand in a drawer.

Jaq and Gus offered to retrieve it. Cinderella agreed but warned them to stay clear of Lucifer the cat. Jaq and Gus did their best to snatch back the wand. Once they got hold of it, the two mice ran as fast as their little legs could carry them.

With a loud *meeeeeeooooooooow!*, Lucifer lunged at the mice.

The Stepmother spun around.
"The wand!" she cried.
But the mice scurried out the
door, still carrying the wand.

The Stepmother called Cinderella a thief and ordered the guards to arrest her. Cinderella and the mice ran through the palace looking for the Prince. When she found him, Cinderella tried to lift the spell, but the Stepmother grabbed the wand.

Cinderella made a desperate plea to the Prince. "You're under a spell," she cried. "That's why you don't remember me."

Cinderella reached out to touch the Prince. He felt there was something familiar about her.

"Poor child. Obviously out of her mind," the Stepmother said. Once the Prince left, however, the Stepmother turned to the head guard and ordered: "Put her on the next ship leaving the kingdom. I want her banished forever."

It was now up to
Cinderella's friends
to save the day. Jaq
and Gus found the
Prince and told him
the truth.

The mice even showed the
handsome prince the glass
slipper that the bluebirds
had meticulously glued
back together.
When the
Prince heard his
true love was on a
ship that was set
to sail, he raced
out the door and
towards the harbor.

The Prince arrived at the ship just in time. As soon as he touched Cinderella's hands, the spell that he was under was broken. The Prince suddenly remembered everything about Cinderella. The Prince asked for her hand in marriage, and Cinderella joyfully accepted.

Together at last, Cinderella and the Prince returned to the palace. Inside, however, the Stepmother was furious. "He thinks he can ruin my plans," she hissed. "I think not!"

As the guards broke through the locked door to arrest the wicked woman and her daughters, the Stepmother waved the magic wand. In a brilliant burst of light, she and her daughters vanished.

As Cinderella prepared that evening for her wedding, her evil stepmother emerged.

"It appears you were right, Cinderella," the Stepmother said coolly. "The Prince does want to marry you—and marry you he shall." Then she called out for Anastasia. Her daughter stepped out of the shadows—looking exactly like Cinderella!

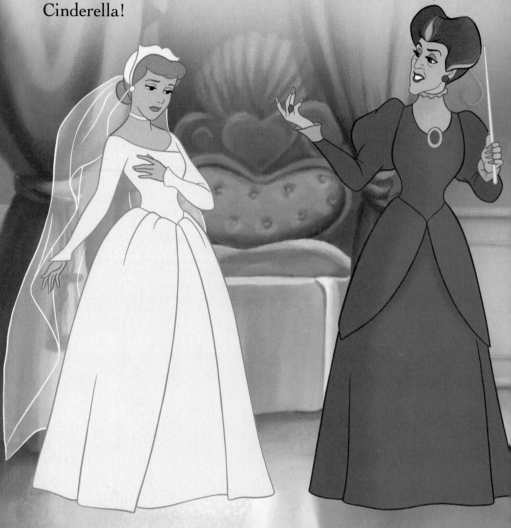

With a flourish, the Stepmother waved the magic wand, and the real Cinderella and the mice disappeared!

They reappeared trapped inside an evil pumpkin coach. The sinister coachman was none other than Lucifer the cat. He had strict orders: get rid of Cinderella once and for all.

Lucifer cracked the whip over the horse's head, and the coach hurtled through the night faster than a shooting star. Cinderella and her friends feared for their lives.

Cinderella needed to do something—and quick. Desperately, she yanked on the vine that Lucifer was sitting on. That sent the cat flying head over paws from the coach into a muddy stream. Gus and Jaq then pulled out the pin that connected the horse's harness to the coach.

Finally, all of the friends were on the horse,
safe and sound. Cinderella grabbed the reins
and pulled the beast to a stop—just in time! The
pumpkin coach plummeted over the cliff's edge.

Determined not to miss her own wedding, Cinderella dashed towards the palace.

"Do you, Cinderella, take this man as your lawfully wedded husband?" the Bishop asked Anastasia.

Anastasia hesitated. She wanted to be loved for who she was, not for who she was pretending to be. "I . . . I . . . don't," she said finally.

At that moment the real Cinderella arrived and ran down the aisle. All the guests gasped in surprise.

　　With Drizella at her side, the Stepmother stormed
out of her hiding place. "Spoiled little ingrate," she
growled at Anastasia.

　　The Stepmother aimed the magic wand at Anastasia
and Cinderella and called out, "Bibbidi-bobbidi-boo!"

　　"No!" yelled the Prince, leaping to protect the young
women. He drew his sword and deflected the wand's
magic power.

　　The magic light from the wand turned the evil
stepmother and Drizella into toads!

Anastasia took the wand and transformed back to her true self. Cinderella thanked her stepsister for acting so honorably and not marrying the Prince.

Finally, it was time to return the wand to its rightful owner. Anastasia and Cinderella said the magical words. And with a "Bibbidi-bobbidi-boo," the Fairy Godmother's statue came to life. Her first order of business was to restore Cinderella's wedding dress.

"Does *anyone* want to marry my son?" the King asked.

Cinderella smiled radiantly. "I do."

"I now pronounce you husband and wife," said the Bishop.

As Cinderella and the Prince kissed, everyone erupted into applause. Then the couple lived happily ever after—again.